Daddy's Girl

by Breena Jacobs

illustrated
by
Neva Austrew

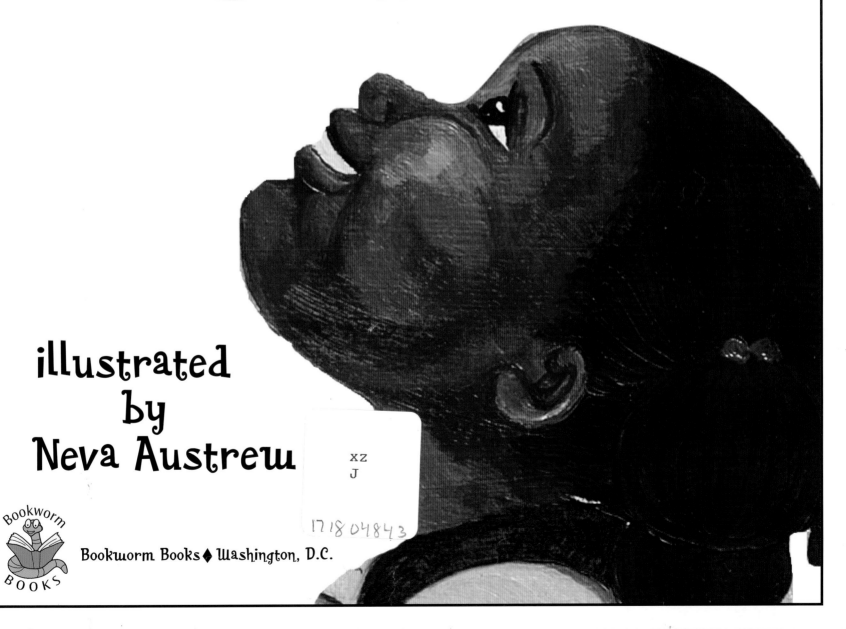

Bookworm Books ◆ Washington, D.C.

Bookworm
BOOKS

www.bookwormbooks.biz

First Edition

Printed in China
Publisher's Cataloging in Publication Data
Provided by Quality Books, Inc.

Jacobs, Breena
Daddy's Girl / Breena Jacobs; illustrated by Neva Austrew.
1st-ed p. cm.
Summary: In rhyming text, a preschool girl delights in the time spent
with her father.

Audience: Ages 2-5
LCCN 2004090900
ISBN   0-9749423-2-4

1. Preschoolers-Juvenile Fiction. 2. Fathers and daughters-Juvenile
fiction. 3. African American fathers-Juvenile fiction [1. Fathers and
daughters-Fiction. 2. African American fathers-Fiction. 3. Stories in
rhyme.] I. Austrew, Neva. II. Title.

PZ8.3.J1372DAD 2004
[E]-QBI-200054

The illustrations for this book are rendered in oil paints on masonite.
The text for this book is set in Baileywick-Festive
Book design by Stonepatch Design

ACKNOWLEDGEMENTS

B.J.

Scott, Kendall and Nya, you inspire me. Thank you for your love and encouragement.

Also, thank you to Him who is able to do exceedingly abundantly above all that we ask or think, according to the power that works in us.
NKJV Ephesians 3:20

N.A.

To my family for your loving support and for being the force behind everything I create.

Mommy leaves early and daddy starts my day. "Rise and shine little princess," my daddy will say.

I jump out of bed to get ready for school.

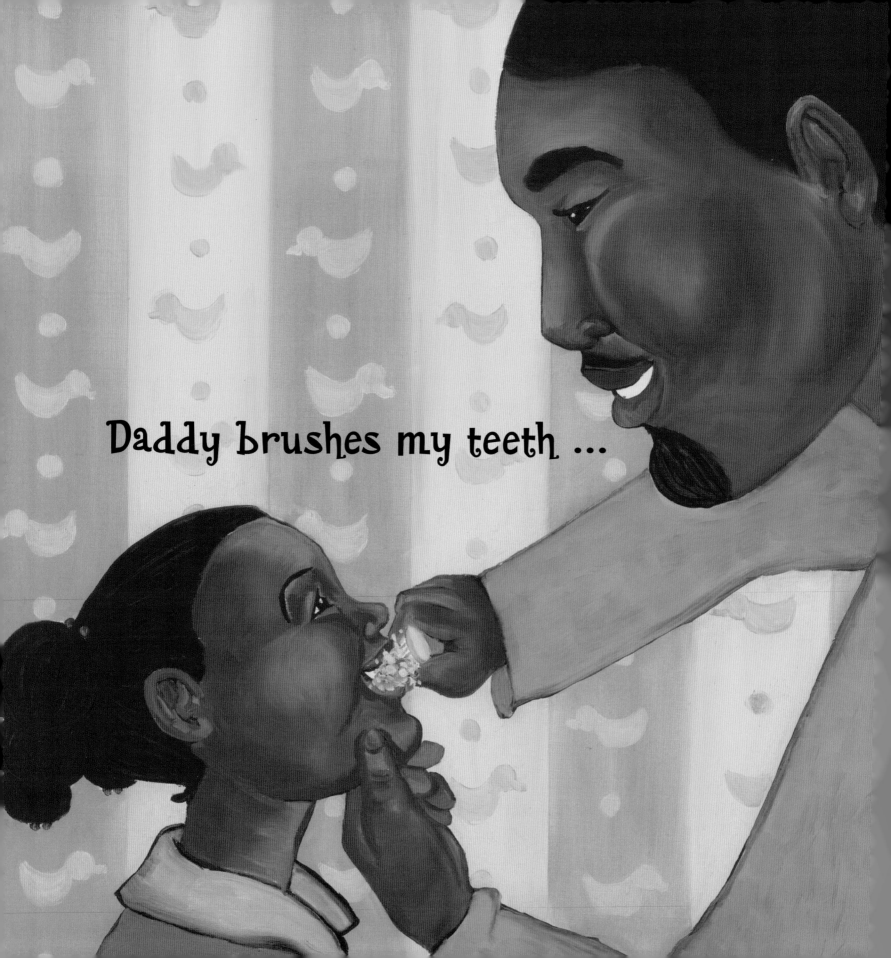

Daddy brushes my teeth ...

while I stand on a stool.

Daddy picks out my clothes while I pick out my shoes. The red ones, the blue ones, which pair shall I choose?

We laugh and we sing as we ride in the car.

When I'm with my daddy I feel like a star.

When I get to school the teacher takes my hand and I kiss daddy goodbye until I see him again.

I feel sad when daddy drives away, because I love him so much and I want him to stay.

Surprise! Surprise!

When I look up, my daddy has come to pick me up!

Daddy, daddy, look what I drew!
I drew a picture of me, and look,
there you are too!

I hug my daddy with all my might.
He hugs me back and squeezes me tight.

After my bath and after I eat, daddy
and I share our favorite treat.

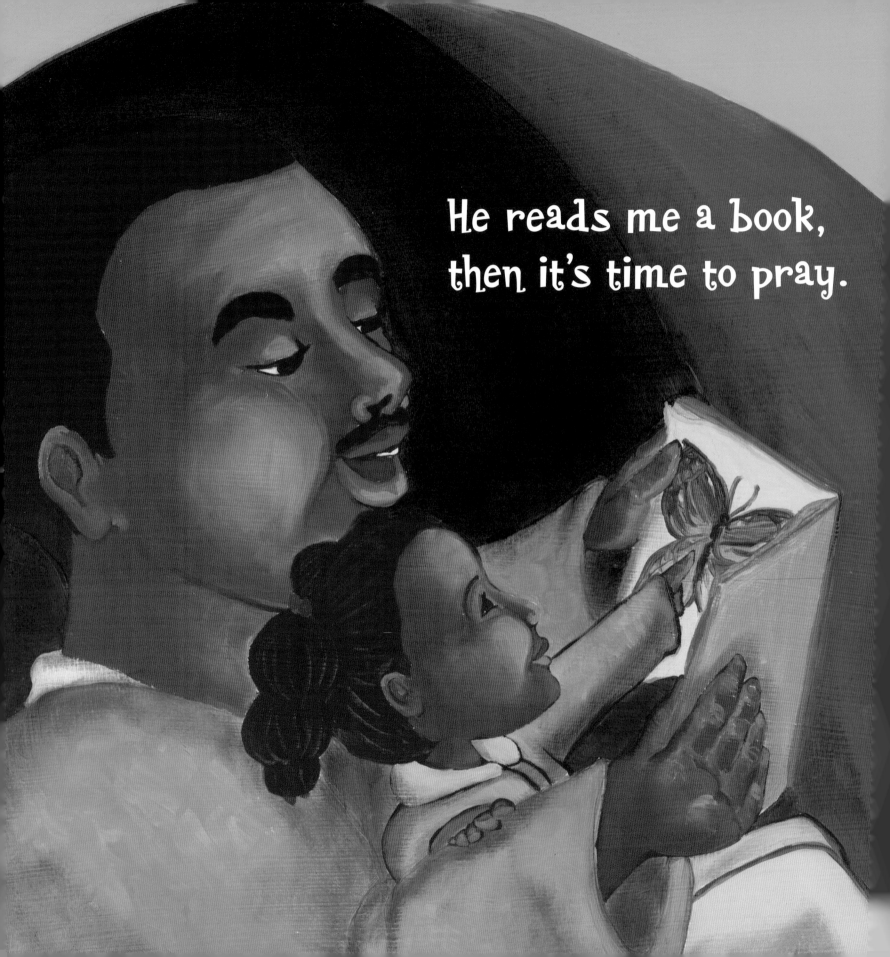

He reads me a book,
then it's time to pray.

Thank you God for this happy day.

He tickles my toes when he tucks me in bed, then he kisses my cheek and then my forehead.

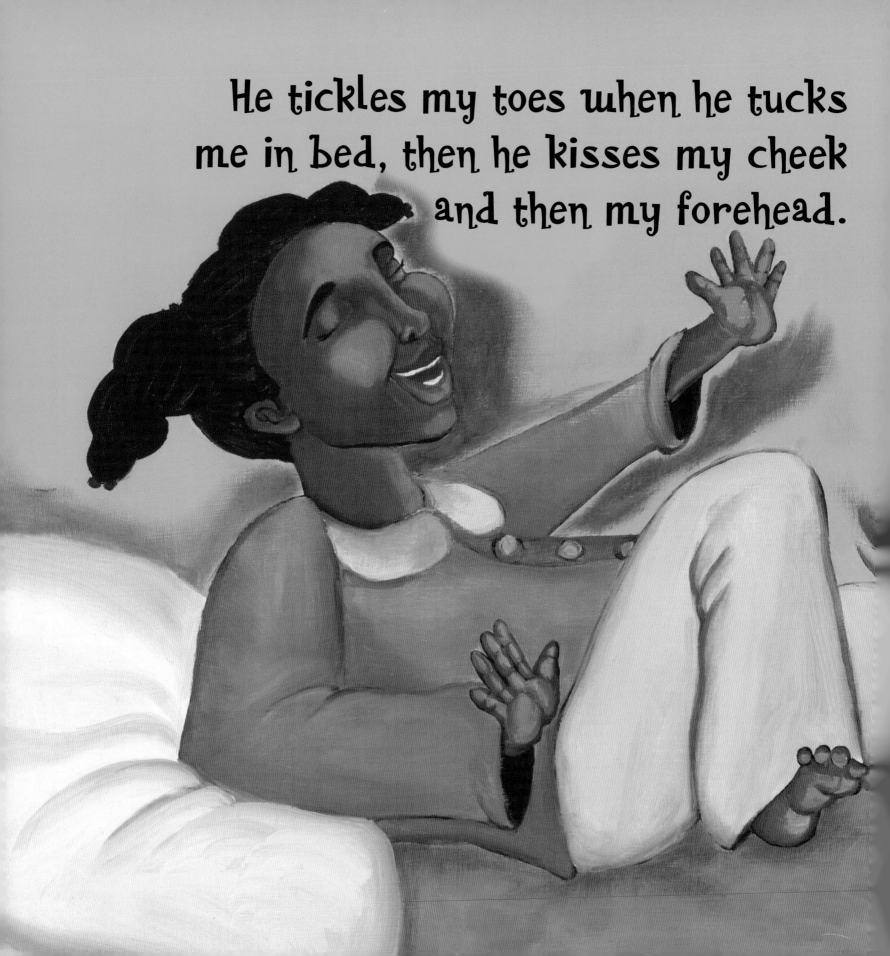

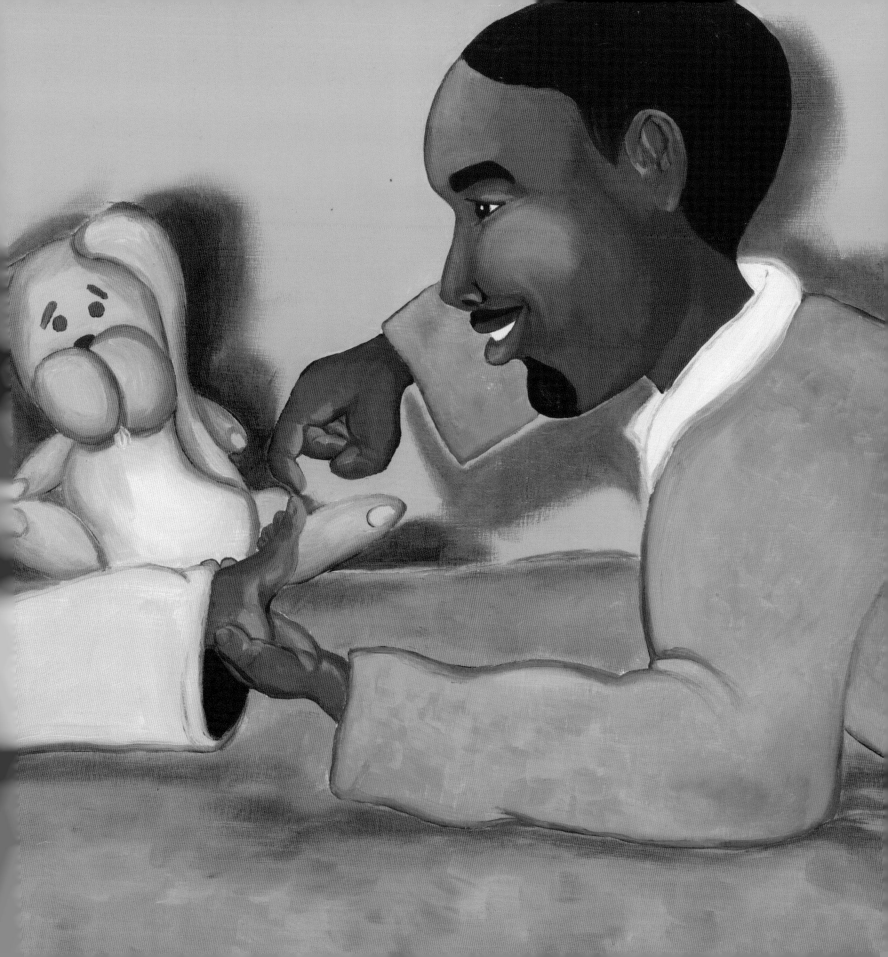

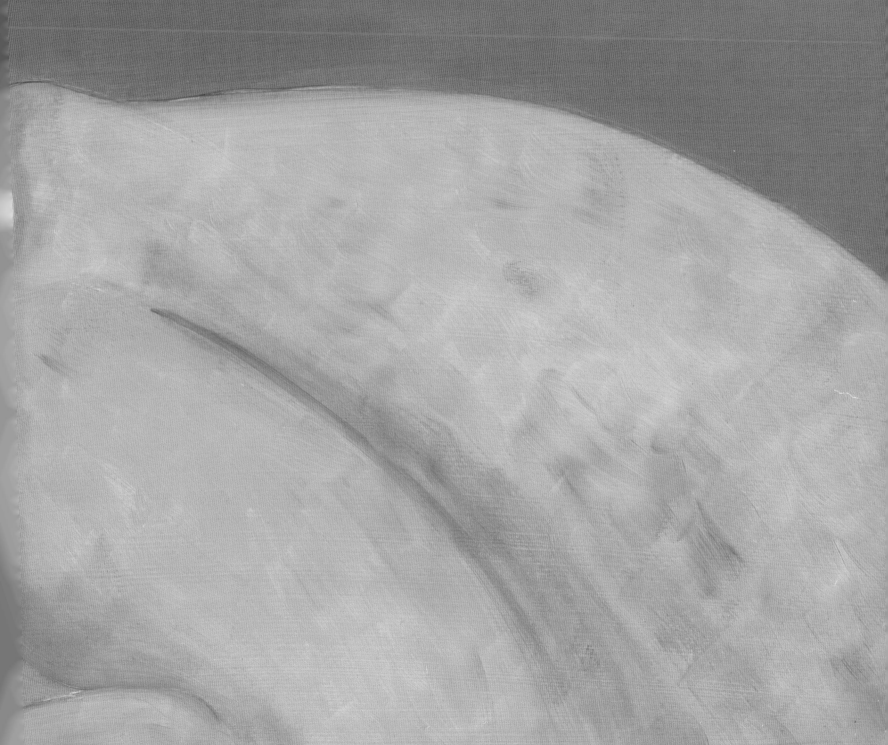

I'm a daddy's girl, can't you see?
I love my daddy and he loves me.